FR

The Best of Arlie Zack

Annick Press gratefully acknowledges the support of The Canada Council

Financial support has been provided from the Lottery Fund by the Government of Alberta through the Alberta Foundation for the Literary Arts

Canadian Cataloguing in Publication Data

Hutchins, H. J. (Hazel J.)
The best of Arlie Zack

ISBN 1-55037-315-3

I. Ohi, Ruth.   II. Title.

PS8565.U74B38 1993   jC813'.54   C93-093079-7
PZ7.H88Be 1993

Trade Distribution in Canada by
Firefly Books Ltd.
250 Sparks Avenue
Willowdale, Ontario M2H 2S4

Educational distribution by
Annick Educational
15 Patricia Avenue
Willowdale, Ont. M2M 1H9

Printed in Canada

THE BEST OF ARLIE ZACK

By Hazel Hutchins

Illustrations by Ruth Ohi

Annick Press, Toronto

Chapter 1

"If I were you I wouldn't even go near the place," said Max. "You don't know the things about Mrs. Spinx that I know." Arlie Zack stood knee-deep in snow at the side of 8th Street and frowned hard at the small white house before him. It wasn't what Max was trying to tell him that made Arlie frown—Max was the kind of kid that just liked to talk a lot—it was the principle of the whole thing.

"Arlie," his mom had said when he'd tried to refuse the shovelling job, "I wish you'd tell me what's wrong. Something's been bugging you for two weeks now and you're taking it out on me instead of..."

"Nothing's bugging me," Arlie had answered. "I'm just not shovelling. If you can't do it the town can get someone else. Period. Double period. Triple period. You can't make me."

His mother's face had shifted through several expressions.

"O.K. Arlie," she had said finally. "I can't make you. No one can make you lift the shovel and push the snow around, but that doesn't mean you get it all your own way either. I know it was goofy of me to climb on the skateboard and break my arm, but if you can't at least fill in for me for a couple of weeks to help out someone who needs help, then that's it. No T.V. No video. No allowance. And you're grounded for as long as there's a flake of snow in this town. But you don't have to do it."

Arlie had stomped down to his bedroom

and slammed the door so hard that the old fishing trophy thumped dully in the secret cubby hole behind his desk.

He'd put on his summer coat, lightest gloves, baseball cap, and sneakers.

And now here he was: Arlie Zack—frozen. Arlie Zack who had just walked two blocks in his sneakers through mountains of snow. He smiled as a cold blast of wind bit even deeper through his summer jacket. They'd be sorry when they found him dead and frozen right in the middle of town. He'd tell them with his last words that he wanted the whole street named "Arlie's Revenge". They'd have to do it too, even if he had only lived here since September, because they'd feel so sorry for him.

"Arlie—are you listening?" Max poked Arlie's elbow with his shovel. "This is important stuff I'm telling you."

Arlie sighed. It was just his special luck that Max Conner lived on the same block as Mrs. Spinx.

"So, I'm trying to tell you, she won't pay," said Max. "She never pays anyone. I get $10.00 every time I shovel in front of the condos around the corner—$15 if the snow's heavy. I do a lot of other houses around here too."

"O.K. She won't pay me," said Arlie.

"And she knows stuff—stuff you wouldn't expect someone to know. Personal stuff," said Max.

"Like what?"

"Never mind," said Max. "I don't want you to know it either."

"You don't make a lot of sense Max," said Arlie.

"And she's mean with her cane. If people don't shovel their walks on this side of town, Mrs. Spinx marches right up to their door and beats on it with her cane. And if that doesn't work she phones the town. My dad says Mrs. Spinx has got more power than the mayor."

"You're a wealth of knowledge, Max," said Arlie.

"I could tell you more, but you wouldn't believe me," said Max. "If I were you, I wouldn't even get started."

"I have to," said Arlie. "Where's her shovel?"

"Over there by her back door. Good luck. You'll need it."

Max headed off down the street. Arlie waded up the walk and picked up the shovel.

Scrape, heave, scrape, heave. There was already snow piled on either side of the walk so he couldn't just push it aside, he really had to work and lift. With all the output of energy he began to realize he probably wouldn't freeze after all, but he was pretty sure his fingers were done for. BOY LOSES THREE DIGITS TO FROSTBITE—MOTHER TO BLAME. That's what the headlines would read.

Scrape, heave, scrape, heave.

He finished the narrow back walk and moved out onto the sidewalk. It was about twice as wide and took about four times as much effort. Even his fingers were beginning to get warm.

Scrape, heave, scrape, heave—all down to the end of the sidewalk he shovelled. At that point Arlie realized something he hadn't quite taken in at first. The house was on a corner. Not only was it on a corner but it wasn't just a single lot on the next side, it was a double lot—twice as long. He had to shovel all the way down to where the trees hung low over the side fence covering what lay beyond!

Arlie frowned so hard his face hurt. Knowing his mother she'd probably gone into the town office and said "I'd like the widest, largest, toughest lot in town to shovel for the winter please—and make sure it's on a corner." Or perhaps, since she'd grown up in this town a long time ago, she'd just asked for Mrs. Spinx's house straight out. His mother was like that. She believed in CHALLENGES in life. She thought Arlie should be like that. His teachers thought he should be like that. The principal thought he should be like that.

As Arlie doggedly shovelled his way around the corner and down what seemed to be the entire length of the next block his whole day played before him. Two "little talks" with teachers. One "little talk" with the principal. "Arlie you're slipping. Arlie you're not concentrating. Arlie we feel you're just not putting in the effort you're capable of. Arlie you…"

Scraaattttcch.

Arlie's shovel skidded out in front of him and almost pulled him face first into the cement. Regaining his balance, Arlie looked up. He had been working so intently he hadn't realized he'd come to the last stretch. He was even more surprised at what he saw beyond the band of overhanging trees. All the walks before him now—other people's walks—were shovelled clear and clean for what seemed to be miles ahead. It was just as Max had said. As Arlie stood looking at this minor miracle he could just hear in the distance the sound of Max's shovel as he worked away on the other side of the house.

With a shiver, Arlie hunched his shoulders and tucked one hand beneath an arm pit as he walked back to the little house to return the shovel. Even stopping for that few seconds had made him cold again—cold enough so that when Mrs. Spinx herself came out of the back door he forgot all about what Max had said and went into an instant daydream about how she was going to invite him in and sit him by the fire and feed him hot chocolate and cookies and then phone the social services and complain about how Sandra Zack wasn't looking after her dear son Arlie.

It was a daydream that didn't come true.

Mrs. Spinx firmly closed the door behind her and stomped down the walk in a pair of no-nonsense winter boots. She was a small lady, as small and old as her house, but there was an air of authority about her. In her hand was the cane, which she seemed to brandish as much as lean on. Her coat was long and dark. Around her head and shoulders was wrapped a great wide scarf of burgundy and gold. From within its folds her face showed the lines and translucent skin of old age, but there wasn't anything meek or feeble about it as she peered out at Arlie.

"Wear warmer clothes next time," she said abruptly. "And don't forget my path to the garbage."

She took his hand out of his armpit and

put something into it. Arlie couldn't see what it was before she closed his fingers over it and his hand was too cold to feel much, but he knew it certainly wasn't one of Max's $10.00 bills. It was something small and hard. Before he had time to look Mrs. Spinx rapped him a few times on the leg with her cane to make him stand aside, and stomped past him down the walk.

Nice lady, thought Arlie, rubbing his shin. He wondered what she'd given him. A nickel? A quarter? He certainly wasn't going to hope for a Loonie.

But when he opened his hand to look, it was even worse than he'd expected. There in the palm of his hand was a brown and green rock. A rock!

Arlie would have chucked it then and there but Mrs. Spinx was thumping along the sidewalk on the other side of the fence and might have come back and hit him with her cane for ingratitude. He shoved the rock in his pocket, dug a quick path to the garbage and left before hypothermia set in.

There was hot cocoa and supper waiting for him when he got home. Arlie was kind of hoping he could start another fight with his mother and get out of this shovelling business forever, but his mom didn't provide him with an opening. She didn't even give a lecture about not wearing enough clothes. She just sat down across the table from him and reached for the ketchup bottle the way she always did.

"Thanks for digging out Mrs. Spinx," she said.

Arlie's mouth was too full of supper to reply.

"What's that beside your plate?" Arlie looked. It was a brown and green rock—the brown and green rock Mrs. Spinx had given him. Funny, he didn't remember taking it out of his jacket pocket. Obviously the cold had numbed his memory.

The rock turned up unexpectedly again while he was doing some of last week's homework. Later he found it beneath the controller on the video games. It wasn't until he hooked one arm around his pillow at bedtime and recognized the feel of it between the folds of the pillowcase, however, that it began to occur to Arlie that there was something strange going on. By then he was so tired from a day of hassles and all the shovelling that he just gave up and fell asleep. Arlie didn't believe in that sort of stuff anyway.

Chapter 2

"Arlie Zack, I don't seem to have your magazine report here."

Mr. Floren, language arts teacher, finished shifting through the pile of paper on his desk and looked up at the milling students he had just dismissed.

"Arlie?"

"I know," said Arlie from where he stood looking out the window.

Mr. Floren tapped his pencil on his desk.

"O.K. Arlie," he said. "What's your excuse this time?"

Arlie didn't answer. Now that they were all on their feet he could see that it was worse outside than he'd thought from watching the flakes come down. A good twelve centimetres of snow had fallen since lunch.

"Arlie..." began Mr. Floren.

Arlie dragged his attention away from the window.

"It's not ready to be handed in because it isn't done," he said.

"Have you started it?" asked Mr. Floren.

"Kind of," said Arlie.

"Have you finished reading the magazine?" asked Mr. Floren. "Mostly," said Arlie.

Mr. Floren frowned.

The trouble with Mr. Floren, thought Arlie, was that he was basically a nice person. You could tell that by the way he frowned instead of started yelling right away. Arlie tried not to frown back. He just wanted to get by without having to explain things. Yes, he'd read the magazine and no, he was not going to write a report about it— but if he said that it would drive Mr. Floren over the edge. So Arlie just waited.

"And you don't even have an excuse? Not even a made up one?" asked Mr. Floren.

"His mother broke her arm."

Jan Markham, smartest kid in Language

Arts class, handed her report across the desk to Mr. Floren and spoke quietly.

"Arlie's mother broke her arm. She was trying to ride Arlie's skateboard but she crashed. Arlie's had to cook dinners and help her with the jewellery she makes and everything all week. He just doesn't like to say."

"Is this true, Arlie?" asked Mr. Floren.

"Sort of," said Arlie.

"You have a one week extension," said Mr. Floren. "One week or you get a big goose egg on the report, Arlie."

Arlie opened his mouth to say something, and closed it again. Better to just let well enough alone, but he was pretty peeved at Jan for butting in. He followed her out of the classroom and down to her locker.

"How'd you know about my mom?" he asked.

Jan was already cranking the tumblers around on her lock. She glanced up at him.

"I'm a medium," she said. "You know... psychic and all that. My professional name is Madame Zelda. I read palms. And tea leaves too. And rings around bathtubs."

Arlie frowned. He didn't know what to make of Jan Markham. At the first of the year he'd thought that anyone who could get 98% on every test she ever wrote was probably about as interesting as an encyclopedia. Lately, however, he wasn't so sure.

"Do you do magazine reports?" asked Arlie, suddenly hopeful.

"No," said Jan. Arlie sighed.

"Arlie," said Jan. "Why don't you just do it yourself? You've been sneaking around with that magazine for weeks—what's it called... 'Outdoor Macho Man' or 'Trout Weekly' or something. You must have read it. So fill in the blanks on the report form. Pretend it's a game—Mr. Floren's game show:

My name is......fill in the blank.

The name of the magazine is......guess that word.

The audience it is aimed at is......

The type of ads are......

Arlie tried to look super pathetic.

"No," said Jan, and turned her back on him.

"Hey Arl!"

It was Max. He was dressed in his heavy knee-high boots, fluorescent jacket and orange toque. Arlie hadn't noticed before but his clothes were a pretty good match for his personality.

"Good snow eh?" said Max.

"Not really," said Arlie.

"Are you going over to Mrs. Spinx's right

away? I have to go over to my dad's office first. Meet you over there later though."

"Don't count on it," said Arlie. "I may not..."

But as usual Max wasn't listening. He was already tramping off down the hall.

"And try and pick up some other business on the way," he called back over his shoulder. "Old Mrs. Spinx is a terror. Doesn't pay either."

Arlie went to his own locker, opened it and tossed his books on the bottom shelf. He reached way in the back on the top shelf and took out "Fishing West"—volume 3. It was the most recent summer issue. Arlie flipped to the article entitled "Raven B.C. to Spurgen Manitoba—10 great fishing stores with hearts (and gear) as big as All Outdoors!" and read it for the 759th time. Something inside him felt like it was falling apart in a million different ways. He closed the book and pushed it back in its safe place. Nope. No magazine report.

*

"C'mon Zack!"

C.J. and Clinton were coming down the hall. Arlie pulled on his jacket, slammed his locker shut and went to meet them.

C.J. and Clinton were the friends Arlie hung around with most often. The three of them walked the long way home together, which meant they went about eight blocks out of their way to hit the candy store. C.J. paid for twenty sours and pocketed about thirty-five. Arlie pretended he didn't notice. If Clinton saw, he didn't say anything either.

C.J. was the leader of their little group. Usually Arlie wasn't much for leaders, but C.J. was different from most. He wasn't mouthy. He didn't brag and act smart. Best of all, he didn't ask Arlie a lot of questions, try to get Arlie to join some team, do things Arlie couldn't afford to do, or ask to come over to Arlie's house. He was always just around. It was easy to follow C.J.

After the candy store, instead of walking along Main Street the way they usually did, C.J. steered them down the back alley behind the Anglican church. They walked in the car tracks where the fresh snow had been packed into geometric patterns that crunched beneath their feet. C.J. and Clinton began trading rotten remarks about Mr. Floren. They were in the other Grade 6 class and when they'd handed in their reports that morning Mr. Floren had decided the entire class had made them too short and they'd all been told to go home and make their reports twice as long for tomorrow. And C.J. had been told to write his out again because it was illegible.

"I'd like to deck him one," said Clinton. "Pow. Plain and simple."

"Well, that's one way," said C.J.

Arlie thrust his hands in his coat pockets and concentrated on being mad at Mr. Floren along with Clinton and C.J. If Mr. Floren hadn't assigned the report in the first place...

If Mr. Floren had told him to do Saturday Night or Cat's World instead of letting him look through the pile...

If Mr. Floren had been a plumber instead of a teacher...

If Mr. Floren and his stupid report would just drop off the edge of the world...

Arlie's thoughts shifted to an object that he'd been absently turning over in his pocket. He took it out and frowned at it. Mrs. Spinx's rock. He knew for certain he hadn't put it in his jacket. Why had his mother put it there? Why would his mother even think twice about a rock? Weird. There it lay covering the palm of his hand, the brown and green twined in an intricate pattern.

"Have you guys ever seen a rock like this?" he asked.

C.J. took the rock and looked it over a bit.

"Zack, you're miles ahead of me," he said. "You know what kind of rock this is, don't you?"

Arlie shook his head.

C.J. looked at the church as if to judge the distance, glanced once around him, and drew back his arm.

"It's a throwing rock," said C.J.

"Wait!" said Arlie.

Too late. The rock went spinning through the air and smacked through the basement window of the church.

"Don't just stand there—run," said C.J.

Arlie ran. Down the alley, around the corner, across the road, and down another alley they went. Arlie would have run clear to Mexico, but C.J. pulled both him and Clinton down to a walk.

"Crumb C.J.!" said Clinton. "What did you do that for?"

"Mr. Floren teaches Sunday school in the basement of the church," said C.J. "I just sent him a present for what he did to us today."

"But what if someone saw us!" said Clinton.

"No one saw us," said C.J. "I checked first—right Arlie?"

Arlie didn't know what to say. It had all happened so fast. One minute they were just talking about being mad at Mr. Floren and the next minute—whack. It was like the candy business. C.J. didn't make a big deal out of stealing a few candies—he just did it. There wasn't a whole lot of choice in this town. If he didn't hang around with C.J. and Clinton, who was he going to hang around with? Arlie's heart was still beating up around his Adam's apple but he tried not to show it.

"I...I don't think anyone saw," said Arlie.

He put his hands in his coat pockets, casual like. There was something hard in his right pocket. In spite of his attempt at inner composure, Arlie felt his heart do a double beat.

"I gotta get home," said Arlie. "Talk to you later."

He took off at a trot before the others could answer, but he didn't go home. He went as far as the park near his house and slowed to a dead stop. He reached in his pocket and pulled out the rock.

How could it be there?

How could he be holding it?

Surely he'd just seen C.J. toss it through the church window with his own eyes!

And yet the whole idea of the rock being in his pocket again didn't scare him. The weight of it in his hand felt only familiar. His rock. Why shouldn't it be in his pocket?

Three more times Arlie tried losing it. Twice it turned up in his pocket again, and once in the palm of his hand.

It was almost dark by the time he got home. Maybe that was why he didn't notice the police car parked outside the apartment building, but once inside the door of number eight he noticed the policeman sitting in his kitchen all right.

He noticed the policeman and gulped.

Arlie and the rock that wouldn't stay lost—were they already on Canada's most wanted list?

Chapter 3

Arlie went down to his bedroom. He closed the door and pushed his bed ahead to block the door. He slid the top left hand drawer of his desk fully open, then lifted it at an angle to unhook it completely. The drawer was shorter than the desk was wide. Behind the runners that guided it into place was a small ledge where the fishing trophy rested.

Arlie reached in and withdrew the small brass statuette. His finger brushed briefly over the name and date.

"It belonged to your dad," Miss Perry had told him the day they visited her in Tri Falls three years ago. "Don't tell your mom, but I've held on to it all these years for you. I found it when I cleaned the things out at the office and I kept it. Your dad's two great loves in life were get-rich-quick schemes and fishing."

"Was he really horrible?" Arlie had asked Miss Perry. "Horrible? Is that what your mother said?"

"No," said Arlie. "She doesn't talk about him at all."

"Well, maybe that's just as well. He gave her some tough times. I should know. I was the secretary. I tried to fix some of their troubles. But...no. He wasn't horrible. I liked him actually. He just...well, he had a funny upbringing with a spinster aunt and I don't think he knew much about family. He thought you were something pretty special—that's a baby picture of you in the envelope he tucked under the fish's tail—but I think the whole idea of him actually being a father scared the living daylights out of him."

Arlie was startled by a tapping on his door.

"Just a minute," he called, quickly putting the statue back in its cubby hole and wrestling with the drawer.

"Mrs. Spinx is on the phone, Arlie," said his mom through the door. "She says you haven't done her walk yet."

Arlie decided this wasn't a good time to argue.

There were prints in the snow all down Mrs. Spinx's walk by the time Arlie got there. They were small, no-nonsense boot prints and a round mark at regular intervals beside them. Mrs. Spinx and her cane had already gone out.

Arlie took the shovel and went to work. It was full dark now—colder but wonderfully quiet. The snow wasn't nearly as deep as yesterday and in no time Arlie was out onto the main sidewalk and rounding the corner. It was almost good to be doing something. He hadn't heard another shovel so he was again surprised as he rounded the corner and saw Max down at the end of the block working his way towards him. Max was using a broom.

"A broom is what you need to finish up right," said Max, walking over to talk. "If I've got time, I like to sweep the walks afterwards. Sometimes I get an extra tip for sweeping. It gets all the little bits you miss with a shovel. It's those little bits that ice up. Mrs. Spinx isn't fond of ice. Hates it worse than snow. Maybe you better borrow my broom."

"No thanks," said Arlie.

Max began sweeping the walk behind Arlie as he shovelled.

"I went up and visited with my dad," said Max. "He was doing a root canal. Root canals make my dad a lot of money but he doesn't like doing them because they're pretty uncomfortable for people. What were you guys throwing rocks at?" Arlie stopped shovelling.

"What rocks?" he asked.

"I saw you from my dad's office. You can see all sorts of things from the dental office. It's the only two-storey building in that part of town. It's the park jobs that really get me. People parallel parking on Main Street—they're always bumping some other car. Front or back. Bump. Crash. You can see the other car move—sometimes as much as a foot—then the driver gets out and pretends it didn't happen. Breaks me up. Bump. Bump. They think nobody sees. They forget there's people above them."

"Did anybody else see?" asked Arlie. "See C.J. and Clinton and me?"

"I don't know," said Max. "They might have. Did you break a window or something?"

"No," said Arlie.

He said it so naturally he almost believed it himself.

"Mrs. Spinx had the little window at the back of her house broken once, the one that leads down to her cellar," said Max. "Somebody tried to break in and rob her while she was away visiting her sister. I guess the guy got in O.K. but he couldn't find his way out again. Got lost in the cellar—or that's what he said. Crazy story, hey. But when the police found him he'd been there a week with nothing to drink but cranberry juice. I guess Mrs. Spinx had 8 cases of cranberry juice left over from her son's wedding 30 years ago or something."

"Max," said Arlie.

"What?" said Max.

"You're weird," said Arlie.

"It's true. Honest. Well, it might not be true but that's the story. I really think you should use the broom," said Max.

"I'll pass," said Arlie. "Thanks anyway. And listen Max, don't say anything to anyone about the rock business."

"If you didn't break a window, what's there to tell?" said Max.

Arlie didn't answer. He hoped Max didn't belong to the Anglican church.

He took the shovel around to the back. He kind of wished Mrs. Spinx was home. Maybe he'd knock on the door. It would kind of cancel out what had happened with the window if he gave the rock back, wouldn't it?

He took it out of his pocket and looked at

it and put it back again. It wouldn't really settle anything. He leaned the shovel against the wall.

That's when he saw the shoe box. It was yellowed with age and dust covered. In one place on top, however, the dust had been brushed away and "Arlie" had been scrawled across the top.

Arlie picked it up quickly, before he could think too much, and headed for home.

"I never knew the sound would be so lovely," said his mother as she cupped her hand around the little conch shell and listened to the sound within. "It's almost like music—terribly sad now and then, plaintive almost, and then wonderfully gay again. How very kind of Mrs. Spinx."

Arlie didn't know what to say. He had listened too, just a moment ago when he'd opened the little shoe box parcel on the kitchen table and removed the conch from its wrapping of old newspaper. The sound he'd heard had been anything but musical. It had been jagged and harsh— almost like fingernails pulled across a blackboard. Well, maybe it wasn't quite that bad, but the undercurrent was there and it wasn't pleasant.

"I sold a couple of pair of earrings today," said his mother. "Lena across the hall bought some for a present and so did Pete."

"Who's Pete?" asked Arlie.

"The policeman who was here," said his mom. "Pete the policeman—how's that for a name? He helped me fix up the clamp from the old bed lamp to use as a vise to hold the jewellery fittings. Now I can work with one hand and actually accomplish something again. Maybe we can make our spring selling tour after all. Won't that be good, Arlie?"

"Sure," said Arlie.

And maybe after that they'd move to the city again, or to an artists' colony in the east, or to Africa. His mother always wanted to go to Africa in a future life—why not now? What did distance mean to her? Didn't she always say that she and Arlie were lucky to have no ties except each other? They could be gypsies!

With a wrenching feeling Arlie realised that possibilities he'd only begun to think about were already moving swiftly out of reach.

Just before going to bed that evening Arlie put the conch to his ear. The sound was definitely like fingers being run across a blackboard.

He buried the conch at the very bottom of his closet under a stack of old clothes, did half a page of his homework from the week before last, and went to sleep.

Chapter 4

"Arlie, you and I have a date after school."

Arlie didn't answer. He just kind of flinched so Mrs. Scott would know he'd heard her. Mrs. Scott was his math teacher. No one left Mrs. Scott's class without KNOWING THEIR MATH. Mrs. Scott said she'd had one student that was in her class for 25 years before he mastered the 9 times table but he finally got smart and now he was president of a major computer corporation. He APPLIED himself and SUCCEEDED. Just like Arlie was going to do by joining her "Math Club"...

"Right Arlie?" asked Mrs. Scott.

It was the kind of question that didn't require an answer.

"Arlie's mom broke her arm."

Jan Markham, smartest kid in math class, leaned across Mrs. Scott's desk confidentially.

"Arlie's had to cook dinner and scrub floors and help his mom with her jewellery all week. And shovel the senior's walk that they take care of. He hasn't had much time to study. He just doesn't like to say."

"I see," said Mrs. Scott.

She frowned at Arlie. Arlie tried not to frown back.

"Well, in that case I'll expect you for a full hour after school Arlie, instead of just half an hour. If you're not finding time for your schoolwork at home, then we'll have to make sure you find time here at school."

"That backfired, didn't it," said Jan as they filed out of class. "Sorry, Arlie."

Arlie just glowered at her and passed by.

For the rest of the day his mood got darker and darker. Arlie wasn't sure if it was the date with Mrs. Scott, the broken window from the night before, or the fact that it was snowing. Again. Three days in a row it had snowed now.

By the time school was over and he went up to Mrs. Scott's room for "Math Club", Arlie was in a very black mood. He swung through the door and sat at the nearest desk. Whack. Someone threw an eraser at him. Arlie scowled and turned around to see who it was. There at the back of the room sat C.J. He motioned to Arlie to come back. Arlie scrambled over a few desks and sat down again.

"What are you doing here?" asked Arlie.

"Are you kidding?" said C.J. "Math Club is where I like most to spend my time."

"Do we really have to keep coming until we pass her tests?" asked Arlie.

"Yup," said C.J. "But don't worry. Mrs. Scott just joined my hit..."

Before he could say more there was the sound of high heels clicking down the hall.

"Hello again everyone," she said as she came through the doorway. "For those of you who haven't been to Math Club before, I want you to know that the half hour you spend here really is going to make a difference. All you do is write out the times tables. I know it's boring— but it works. Write them a whole line at a time...not in rows. At the end of the study time we'll do the test. You have to get 100 questions done in three minutes with no more than five wrong." Arlie scowled even harder. It would take him three weeks to get his math facts as fast as she wanted them. And what had C.J. been going to tell him? And it was still snowing. Big flakes. Big heavy flakes.

As Arlie wrote out his stupid tables, his mood became blacker and blacker. He failed the timed test which meant he'd have to stay again next Math Club day. And then as everyone else left the room, Mrs. Scott came to stand by his desk.

"All right, Arlie," she said. "You can get out your regular homework now, I want it done before you leave tonight as well."

All alone in the class, except for Mrs. Scott working at her desk way up front, Arlie opened the page of problems Mrs. Scott had written out for the class homework. He read the first question and blinked. He read it again.

"It is a 135 kilometre bus ride from here to the town of Raven, B.C. The one way fare is $12.95. There is a 20% reduction if you buy a two way ticket. What is the price of a two way ticket? If the bus averages 90 kilometres per hour, how long will it take you to make the one way trip?"

Arlie stared at the problem and read it yet again. Mrs. Scott always used real figures and real places in her math problems. She said it made much more sense than figuring out problems about things that had nothing to do with you.

In Arlie's case she was particularly correct. Arlie bent to work and figured out the problem. Then he checked it. And rechecked it. $20.72. A one and a half hour trip. All he needed was $20.72! He was sure he had that much money at home.

Arlie forced himself to finish the rest of his homework and earn dismissal. From the school he walked straight to Mrs. Spinx's house. He was almost looking forward to the shovelling now. As he worked he turned things over in his head—how much money he'd need, where to find out the bus schedule. When. When.

He was almost disappointed when he finished the walk and found that Max wasn't there to meet him. Max probably knew the bus schedule, he knew everything else. And Max seemed close to his dad.

Mrs. Spinx was framed in the doorway of her house when Arlie came up the back walk to put the shovel away.

"Your mother would like to speak to you on the phone," she said. "Mind you, leave your boots in the porch." And she turned and went inside herself.

Arlie hesitated. He wasn't sure he wanted to go into Mrs. Spinx's house. As he stood there Mrs. Spinx poked her head out again.

"Greasy grimy gopher guts," she said.

Arlie felt himself turn red. When he'd been a little kid those had been the code words he and his mother had thought up in case someone he didn't know very well had to pick him up from kindergarten. If she had told Mrs. Spinx to use it, the phone call must be important. He walked into the porch, took off his boots, and stepped into the little house proper. "Arlie, it's Mom."

The voice had a hollow sound as if she was phoning from a tin drum.

"Listen, nothing's really wrong and I'm just fine, but I'm at the hospital. For some reason this broken arm business has got my sugar level and insulin and everything all mixed up. They want me to stay in overnight. It's not a big thing but everybody says if I stay here tonight and get stabilized it'll save me ending up in here for a couple of days later on. Mrs. Spinx has been kind enough to say you can stay at her house."

Arlie couldn't believe what he was hearing.

"Just for tonight, Arlie. She knows all about boys. She has four sons of her own. Arlie?"

"I could stay with Lena across the hall," said Arlie.

"Lena's out of town."

"I could stay by myself," said Arlie.

"No," said his mother. "I want you to stay with someone. Actually you have a choice. Pete gets off shift in an hour and he said he could pick you up and take you to his place. Would you rather do that?"

Pete. Pete the policeman.

"No," said Arlie. "I'll...I'll stay here."

"I know it'll be strange, Arlie, but you'll be O.K. Mrs. Spinx is nice, Arlie."

Arlie didn't answer.

"Listen Arlie, if there's anything wrong, just tell me. If there's something wrong I'll make them let me out of here and I'll come get you."

Arlie knew it was important to tell his mother the truth. She hated hospitals and wouldn't be there if she didn't have to be.

"No," said Arlie. "I'll be O.K."

"Look, they're calling me and I'd better go. I'll phone you, O.K.? Later. Love you. And don't worry."

"Bye," said Arlie.

He waited until he heard the click of the receiver hanging up at the other end, and then he put the phone back in its cradle. He looked around him with a very weird sensation. Home for the night.

Chapter 5

There was toast with cheese melted on top and tinned soup for supper. For dessert there was apple sauce. It felt more like lunch than supper to Arlie, but it could have been a whole lot worse and as he sat at the table—his shovelling finished, his coat and pack sack hung above his boots in the back porch—he began to think he might survive after all.

He watched Mrs. Spinx move about the kitchen. His mother was right—Arlie wasn't used to old people. He knew it wasn't polite to stare but he couldn't help being interested. When his mother made supper, she went crashing and banging around the kitchen at a million miles an hour. Mrs. Spinx just did things kind of quietly and slowly. Her pots and pans were worn to a smooth, purposeful softness. The plates she handed to Arlie to put on the table were big and heavy, the patterns faded. The knives had bone handles. The spoons were heavy and large.

She handed Arlie two tea cups to put on the table. When they had finished eating— silently, except for things like "would you like more," and "please pass the salt"—Mrs. Spinx filled Arlie's cup with hot water and her own with tea. She added sugar and cream to both. Then, while Arlie sipped the warm sweetness from his cup she poured hers into her saucer and drank from it. Arlie knew he was staring outright now.

"When you're 210 years old, you can do what you like," said Mrs. Spinx. "It's one of very few advantages."

"No one's 210 years old," said Arlie.

Mrs. Spinx lifted an eyebrow and continued to slurp her tea.

She made him dry the dishes. While he did so, she told him the history of each plate and knife and tea cup. Arlie didn't know what to say and he was afraid if he said something wrong she'd stop talking and he didn't want her to stop. It made him feel better when she talked. She became more real, more like other people he knew who weren't 210. Arlie had noticed that about people before. At first they were just their physical parts pieced together, but when they started talking—well, everything changed somehow, like a million doors opening. Sometimes you liked what was behind the doors, sometimes you didn't. He couldn't tell with Mrs. Spinx yet. She seemed to have more doors than most.

As they put the last of the dishes away, Mrs. Spinx turned to him.

"That will be your mother," she said. "When you've finished talking, bring your homework into the living room."

A moment later the phone rang. Yes, it was his mother. Weird.

If the kitchen was small and neat, the living room was enormous and messy. Rambling. Rolling. Old furniture and big deep chairs. Pictures in dark frames. Lamps with shades of rose and green. Knickknacks everywhere. Rugs on rugs. A desk stacked high with papers. An easy chair surrounded by books and magazines. In one corner was an easel with an incomplete painting—like a thought half-formed. On a low table a plaster-of-paris desert landscape with fishbone cacti and peach-pit hills and clove stems sticking out like the bones of some poor lost wanderer. On a higher table were the pieces of a jigsaw puzzle. It was the puzzle that drew Arlie.

"Homework first," said Mrs. Spinx. "Mind the stove."

There was a little wood-burning stove not far from the easy chair in which Mrs. Spinx was knitting. Arlie sat down on the floor on the other side of it and drew in the warmth and did enough bits and pieces of homework to get him through the next day without too much hassle.

"Not much of a talker, are you," said Mrs. Spinx.

Arlie didn't know what to say to that. He was beginning to feel uncomfortable again.

"Can I try the puzzle now?" he asked.

"I think so," said Mrs. Spinx.

Arlie settled into the chair by the table. He looked around for the lid of the box but couldn't find it.

"Is there a picture to work from?" he asked.

"Not really," said Mrs. Spinx.

"What's it supposed to be?" asked Arlie.

"I don't know. I've been working on it for years but I never quite seem to get it right," said Mrs. Spinx.

Arlie shrugged and began fitting pieces together. It went a lot faster than he expected, considering he didn't have a picture to go by. For about an hour he worked—not really thinking about what he was doing. Just fitting pieces together that matched shape and small details—lines that carried on from piece to piece, colours that melded together. When he had finished, he wasn't even aware of what he'd put together until he drew back and looked at it.

It was a man, a man in a business suit, not a front view, but seen from behind, walking, walking away from the viewer. And before him, incongruously, was a beach—a tropical beach...blue sky and sparkling water. The man was stepping onto the sand, walking away, walking away.

Arlie felt the queasiest feeling in his stomach. He knew the picture, not from something he'd seen but from deep inside him. His father. That was how Arlie had always imagined him. Walking away. Dissolving from this life into some other exotic and safe refuge, away, away.

But the picture wasn't true any more. Arlie knew that. He took the pieces apart and tried to put them together differently. What was the town of Raven like? Hills? Almost mountains? Trees. Trees. And the Market Square where the store was. Fishing tackle. Nets. Hip waders. Maps. Hand-tied flies. And what would he be wearing? A plaid shirt? Blue jeans? His face, what would it look like? Like Arlie's? Like the pictures in the photo album at home? Like a stranger's?

Some of the pieces went together easily, but others did not...would never go together. That was why Arlie needed to go and see. Himself. Just to see. It didn't matter if the man whose face wouldn't emerge from the puzzle didn't know who he was. It didn't matter if he didn't even speak to Arlie. Just to see him would be enough. Because he might not be there next year. Or Arlie might not be here. They might never be this close again. Arlie didn't want to start anything or solve anything or ruin anything. He just wanted to see. He understood that now in a way he hadn't before.

How could he ever explain that to his mom?

A noise behind Arlie seemed to wake him as if from a dream. Mrs. Spinx had opened the little stove and was moving the coals around with a poker. The sofa had been made into a bed, the top blanket turned back invitingly. Arlie padded down the hall to the washroom, came back in his long johns and T shirt, and climbed between the sheets which were warm from the fire. The old lady was moving quietly around the room clicking off lamps. She was a strong figure still, but more approachable in the soft light.

"Mrs. Spinx?"

"Yes Arlie."

"Did someone really break into your basement and get lost down there for three weeks and live on nothing but cranberry juice?"

"Who did you hear that from?"

"Max. Max Conner."

"Ah, yes. Max. I'm very fond of Max, but don't you ever tell him that. It would ruin his fun completely."

"Did they really get lost down there for three weeks?"

"Oh well, yes. That's what the man said, but I don't know how much of it one can believe because he was a very foolish type of man. He broke the window for a start. He didn't even bother to see if it was locked, which it wasn't. He could have just pried it open and climbed in. Anyone still could if they wanted to. Some people are very foolish. They make things so much more complicated that they need to be."

She reached down to the chair where she had been knitting, picked up something and laid it beside Arlie's clothes.

"What's that?" asked Arlie sleepily.

"Just a toque," said Mrs. Spinx. "Not very exciting for a twelve year old boy, I'm afraid. But perhaps..."

Chapter 6

The big news at school the next day was that someone had egged Mrs. Scott's house last night. Arlie heard it but it didn't really register. He had other things to think about, and besides, he didn't have math until later. He had science.

A.M. Vanderguard taught science. Vanderguard was the single teacher in the school that Arlie couldn't stand. He was pompous. He was sarcastic. He played favourites with those he liked, and picked on those he didn't. As far as Arlie could tell the only reason he was a teacher at all was because he liked playing king. It was just at the end of the period that he called Arlie to stand up in front of the class.

"Mr. Zack, before I hand out these test results I want you to witness personally that I put your name on the list of people who are officially flunking science," said Vanderguard.

As Arlie watched, Vanderguard turned to the board and wrote "Zack" in the upper left-hand corner. Arlie noticed that two other names had been added to the list since yesterday. Both names were from the other grade 6 class. One of the names was C.J.'s.

"Now, doesn't that feel good?" asked Vanderguard. "Doesn't that feel uplifting, Zack? Doesn't it feel splendid to see how totally dense you really are?"

Arlie didn't even try not to frown back. Out of the corner of his eye he saw Jan Markham, smartest kid in science class, bite the top of her pencil, but she didn't say a word either. A.M. Vanderguard rubbed his hands together and smiled.

"Class dismissed—winners and losers."

"Vanderguard is a pin-head," said Jan, coming up behind him as they filed into the hall.

Arlie didn't answer. He hadn't much liked being dragged up to the front of the class to have his name put on the board, but it didn't bother him as much as it would have even yesterday. Today Arlie had plans to make.

C.J. was going into the next classroom. Jan dragged Arlie over in his direction.

"Clarence, did Vanderguard call you up in front of the whole class to put you on his list?" she asked.

"Sure," said C.J. "Me and Vanderguard are pals. I'm pals with all the teachers." He winked at Arlie. "Watch out for Mrs. Scott. Someone egged her house last night. She's on the war path."

Arlie opened his mouth to say something, but C.J. just smiled innocently and slid into the classroom. Arlie turned back to his own concerns.

The bus went west through town at 7:45 in the morning; he'd found that out on his way to school this morning.

He'd need an excuse to leave for school early—that was easy.

He'd need a note for school to say why he was away—trickier, but he figured he could manage it.

He'd need...

"Hey, what are you doing?"

Arlie had hardly noticed that Jan had followed him to his locker. Now she was rummaging around in his books.

"I'm going to help you," said Jan.

"You're what?"

"I'm helping you. I'm going to tutor you," said Jan.

"No, you're not," said Arlie.

"Yes, I am. I'm going to look over your work and find out what you're doing wrong and cure you."

"Jan!"

"I like you. Nobody I like can be as stupid as the teachers make you out to be. They're missing something. Maybe you're dyslexic. Or maybe..."

"I'm not dyslexic. I'm hopeless. It's simple. Give me back my boo..."

"Tomorrow," said Jan. "I've left you your math for last period, but you won't need the rest until tomorrow. It's not like you do your homework anyway."

"Hey Arl!" Max stepped in between them, larger than life. "I don't believe it. You're alive!"

"Max—move," said Arlie, as Jan reached far in the top shelf to get the last of his books.

"You stayed the night in the Spinx house and you're still alive. And you still talk. And walk," said Max.

"Max!"

Arlie couldn't believe it. Jan had taken the Fishing West magazine.

"How did you manage it? What's she like? Did she show you her basement?"

"Look, Max," said Arlie, really looking at Max and trying to get through to him so he'd move and let him by. "She's not quite what you think she is. She's not quite the way I thought she was either. She's just different. She's O.K.... but different. I'll tell you all about it later. I promise. Now please move," said Arlie.

Max stepped aside. Arlie hurried down the hall in the direction Jan had taken. By the time he turned the corner, however, she was already out of sight. The hallways were clearing rapidly and he still had to change into his gym shorts.

It's all right, Arlie told himself. It's all right. I know what I need to know. The magazine doesn't matter. If I go running all over after Jan, I'll only draw attention to everything. It's all right. Maybe I can even get it back in math class.

Arlie had forgotten about Mrs. Scott being on the war path, and she definitely was. Math class began with a ten minute lecture on "Responsibility and Maturity" and the idea that if people had a complaint with her they were welcome to bring it out in the open, up front, and they'd deal with it. They'd deal with it privately between them, or with someone from the office, or with an ombudsman of the student's choosing. But sneakiness—mindless egg-throwing sneakiness—proved nothing and was not to be tolerated.

Mrs. Scott was in wonderful form and Arlie couldn't help but admire her. She was that kind of teacher. She drove you crazy but you admired her because she was open about it. You knew where you stood with her and you knew it was the same for everyone in the class. Frankly, Arlie was pretty mad that someone would egg her house to start with. He kind of wanted to tell her so and he might have, too, except she got to him first.

Halfway through class he found her standing by his desk.

"Arlie, there's no Math Club today, but if there's anything you want to talk to me about after school I'll be here," she said quietly.

As she drifted away, Arlie began to realize what she meant. The egg throwing—she thought he was responsible! A couple of kids near him were giving him funny little glances. Did they think he was responsible too? Because he'd been kept after class? Because he was the new kid in town? Well, he wasn't responsible, but he had a sickening feeling that he knew who was.

I'm not going to think about it, Arlie told himself. I didn't do it and I'm not going to think about it. It's not my concern.

He didn't look at anyone or talk to anyone for the rest of the class. After school he somehow managed to avoid Max and Jan and even C.J. and Clinton on his way home.

I'm not involved with any egg-throwing, thought Arlie, as his mother told him about her night in the hospital and asked how it had been with Mrs. Spinx.

Broken windows have nothing to do with me, thought Arlie, as he ate supper and washed the dishes.

Anything else that happens is not my concern, thought Arlie firmly as he walked down the hall to his bedroom. But there it stopped. As soon as he got into his room, he could hear it. The conch. Even buried under layers of dirty clothes he could hear it—its horrible grating noise, loud and whining and grating. He dug it out from the back of the closet. I'll break it, he thought. I'll break it and that will stop the sound.

But once he held it in his hands he could no more break it than jump out a tenth-storey window. It was beautiful. Its only fault was that it told people things—told them how they really felt inside.

Arlie went out to the living room. "I need to go out," he told his mother. "I need to talk to a friend about something."

"Sounds important. I'd be glad to listen if you just need an ear to talk to," said his mother.

"I can't," said Arlie. "But I'm not getting into trouble or anything. I promise. An hour."

His mother nodded and Arlie put on his boots and jacket and headed out the door. He didn't even bother to stop at C.J.'s house, or at Clinton's. He just headed down by the river where he knew one of the big brick houses belonged to A.M. Vanderguard.

Chapter 7

The river by winter moonlight rolled along sleekly, with islands of ice riding like ghosts upon its dark current.

Arlie walked upstream along the dike. He was sure this was the way C.J. would come, but he wasn't sure if his timing was right or even which house was Vanderguard's. As he crouched in the shadows by a stone wall where he could see in either direction, he felt very much alone. He was beginning to have doubts. What was he doing here anyway? Why should he be worrying about Vanderguard?

Putting his hands in his pockets his fingers touched the small rock that lay quietly within.

His rock. There, waiting alone in the darkness, it felt like the very centre of his being, the little core that was the real Arlie and could never be lost. That was important...oh, not the rock itself, but that simplest sense of self that somehow meant there were other things too, ideas like right and wrong and now and the day after now when you still had to live with yourself.

Maybe I'm not here for Vanderguard after all, thought Arlie.

That's when he saw movement along the dike. There were two of them, C.J. and Clinton. Arlie hadn't been sure about Clinton. They slid down off the dike, too far away for Arlie to call them. Arlie went after them, down into the darkness of a yard with a big house and a wide driveway. He lost sight of them for a moment and then picked them up again in the driveway, crouched by a car. They were watching so intently they didn't notice Arlie until he was practically beside them.

"C.J., Clinton."

Arlie saw both of them jump.

"It's me, Arlie."

"Crumb, Arlie," said Clinton.

"Get down and be quiet," said C.J.

Arlie crouched down and came closer.

"What are you doing?" asked Arlie.

"What do you think," said C.J., holding up a small bag in the darkness. "Surprise for old Vanderguard. A nice sweet gas tank."

"Look C.J., this is dumb," said Arlie. "You're going to get all of us in a lot of trouble."

"I told you it was just as well we couldn't find him last night," said Clinton.

"I thought you were on our side, Zack. What gives?" said C.J.

"I just think it's dumb, that's all. It doesn't prove anything."

"So if you don't like it, get lost," said C.J.

"I can't. Everyone thinks I'm in on it," said Arlie.

"Then I guess you are," said C.J. "Here, hold this bag of sugar while I get the gas cap."

C.J. plunked the sugar in Arlie's hands and reached across to unscrew the cap. Arlie froze. He didn't know what to do. He'd thought if he was there, they'd just stop. That's all. Just stop. But here he was holding the sugar and Clinton was opening it and C.J. had the cap off the gas tank and was reaching for it.

"STOP MURDER POLICE," shouted Arlie. "FIRE AVALANCHE EARTHQUAKE AIR RAID WEEEEEE-OOOOOOO WEEEEEEE-OOOOOO!"

Someone looked out a window next door. A light came on on Vanderguard's porch.

C.J. split left.

Clinton split right.

There was Arlie, alone, standing by the car with a bag of sugar in his hands and making siren sounds.

I'm crazy, thought Arlie.

He dropped the sugar and ran. Behind him he heard Vanderguard's voice in the darkness.

"I see you. Don't think I don't know who you are. You'll pay for this!"

Arlie didn't stop running until he was all the way back to his apartment building. Even then he didn't go in. He paced back and forth on the front walk and tried to calm down.

I didn't do anything.

I didn't do anything.

In fact, I stopped something from happening, he told himself over and over.

But who was going to believe him? And had Vanderguard really seen who he was in the darkness? And what were C.J. and Clinton going to do to him? He'd just turned his best friends into his best enemies. All for Vanderguard. For dumb old Vanderguard.

"Arlie, is that you?"

Arlie turned to see Jan Markham coming down the steps from the apartment.

"I dropped your books off. I thought you might want to do some homework after all."

She leaned against the railing and looked at him.

"And besides, I know why you don't want to do your magazine report," she said.

"What do you mean, you know," said Arlie. "You don't know anything about me."

"Your Dad's in one of the articles...the one about the fishing store in Raven."

Arlie didn't say anything.

"It's a small town, Arlie," said Jan. "Or at least it was a small town when your mother grew up here. The old timers, like my grandmother and her friend Mrs. Spinx, keep track of things. Your mom was a Simpson. She married some guy named Curly Zack—not exactly a common name. I guess he was a real fishing nut...but he was also a lawyer, a crooked lawyer. Just after your mom and he moved down east, and you were born, some real estate scam your dad was part of fell apart and he ran out on the two of you."

"Thanks a lot, Jan," said Arlie.

"I'm sorry. I don't know how to say it properly. I don't even know if it's true or not," said Jan. "Is it?"

"I guess so," said Arlie.

"But you didn't know he was living out here, did you," said Jan.

"I didn't even know he was in the same country," said Arlie. "I thought he was somewhere else. I mean Mom has never really talked about it but I always thought he had to leave the country and was somewhere...safe, I guess. I thought he couldn't come back or they'd put him in jail. I thought that was why we never heard from him—because he didn't want the police to be able to trace him."

"Does your Mom know he's so close?" asked Jan.

Arlie didn't answer.

"Why don't you ask her?" asked Jan.

Again, Arlie didn't answer.

"Are you afraid she won't let you go see him?"

"No," said Arlie defiantly. "And besides, I am going to go see him. Tomorrow morning, on the bus."

"Does your Mom know?" asked Jan.

"Of course she does. She's paying for the ticket," said Arlie.

He was looking straight across at Jan in the darkness now. She looked levelly back at him.

"Well, isn't that a coincidence," was all she said. "My mother is paying for a ticket for me to go visit my Grandmother in Bentley tomorrow. We'll be on the same bus."

Before Arlie could answer, she turned and walked away down the street, softly through the winter's night.

Chapter 8

"I think he'll be tall. He looks tall in the pictures. I'm pretty tall myself."

They were the first words Arlie had spoken in over an hour. Jan looked up from the book she was reading and glanced out the window of the bus. They were travelling, now, through rugged, tree-covered country where winter lay deep on all sides. Below them the road twisted and turned down to a bridge which it traversed before climbing the other side of the valley.

"That's Sheep Creek," she said. "Sheep Creek, then Beargrass Campground, then Spencer's Lookout, Tyler's Creek, and the municipality of Raven. Not far now."

"How do you know all the names?" asked Arlie.

"Whenever I make this trip I memorize them. You know me. I can memorize anything—math equations, capital cities, kings of England. Do you want to know all the kings and queens of England from the year zero? I memorized them from the back of a ruler I found. Get it—a ruler with rulers on the back?"

Arlie was unresponsive. Jan sighed.

"Well, I could recite them if anyone needed to hear them, which they don't. You know, sometimes I wish I could stop myself—stop myself being so smart. It's fun, but it kind of gets in the way sometimes."

"I don't even know if I'll be able to find him," said Arlie.

"If you do, are you going to tell him who you are?" asked Jan.

"I don't know," said Arlie.

He lapsed again into silence. The bus droned on, eating up the miles. When they had first climbed aboard in the cold darkness of morning it had seemed to travel too slowly. Now it was travelling too fast. Hold it, Arlie wanted to say. Hold it. Slow down and let me get my bearings.

Nine o'clock. At school they'd be doing Language Arts. Then recess, then Vanderguard's class. What if Vanderguard really had recognized him? And what about Clinton and C.J.? It was all one big mess and Arlie didn't want to have to face it. Maybe, he thought, just maybe I won't have to.

"This is it," said Jan, and almost at the same moment the bus began to slow down, moving into the outside lane to take the turn-off.

West of the road it was a lumber town, but down the route the bus took it had a definite tourist-town look—pine trees and snow and rows of motels and a lake that stretched to the hills beyond. In between there were car dealers and service stations, a school, a church and a long row of stores that was Main Street where the bus pulled in to stop. Arlie took a deep breath. He said a quick good-bye to Jan and got off the bus. And there he stood, alone.

Don't think. Don't think.

But it wasn't so easy for Arlie to ignore his own feelings these days. The image of the conch filled his mind and he couldn't help listening.

I'm terrified, thought Arlie, absolutely terrified. Oddly enough, admitting it made him feel better. He supposed pure fear was a lot easier to handle than some of the more confusing emotions he'd been feeling lately.

"I think the hotel over there is the main hotel and bus depot. Let's ask there."

Arlie turned. Jan was standing behind him.

"Stop-over privileges," she explained. "I'll get the next bus. Gram's not expecting me until supper."

Arlie looked at her suspiciously, but didn't speak.

The man at the hotel desk was tall and fair and Arlie didn't like him much. He wouldn't answer their questions—just kind of looked at them, and rolled his cigarette from one corner of his mouth to the other, and said they were too young for the beer parlour. He seemed to think he'd made some great witty joke and broke into a wheezy laugh.

They walked across the street to a hardware store and got directions to Market Square. It was a few blocks away, down at the other end of Main Street. As they drew near it the town grew quieter and quieter, and Jan shook her head.

"I've got a funny feeling about this, Arlie," she said.

Market Square was deserted. The shops were closed. Arlie was standing exactly in front of Curly's Fishing Palace but the windows were boarded over and even the "Gone Fishing" sign on the door seemed to have an abandoned look.

"What's wrong?" asked Arlie.

"It's a summer place," said Jan, reading a

sign on one of the buildings. "Open May to September. We should have known that. The tourist industry around here is a summer business, Arlie. We should have..."

"But maybe he's still around," said Arlie. "Maybe he still stays in town over the winter."

"We could ask for him by name at the hardware store," said Jan.

Arlie shook his head.

"I don't want anyone to know...well, to know that I'm looking for him in particular," he said.

Disappointment settled hard upon them as they looked around the deserted square; then Arlie's eye fell upon a familiar blue booth.

"Let's try the phone book," he said.

Curly Zack was in the phone book all right, and so was an address. Arlie and Jan got directions again and walked up the hill above town to a small house that had been divided into two even smaller halves. There was obviously someone living on the side in which they were interested, but tire tracks in the snow showed that the car that regularly parked there had pulled out earlier that morning.

There was a little kids' play park across the street. Arlie climbed to the top of the slide there and sat looking at the house.

"Now what?" asked Jan.

"We wait. For now, at least, we wait. Probably he's just gone somewhere for a little while and he'll come back. It's warm. I'll sit here in the park and wait. I've got all day," said Arlie.

"No you don't," said Jan.

Arlie looked at her. A feeling of anger began to grow inside him. He was pretty sure he understood. "You told, didn't you!" he said. "You told someone!"

"I didn't exactly tell. I just left a note for ny mom, just in case we got in trouble. She won't find it until she comes home at noon and...well, she might not even phone your mom at all. I had to tell her where I was going, Arlie."

"I thought she knew where you were going! I thought she was sending you to your grandmother's!" said Arlie.

"And I thought your mom was sending you here to see your dad, so how could I be telling on you!" said Jan.

Arlie put his lips together, hard. He was mad. He was really mad. Everything was ruined. Completely ruined. He was so mad his head hurt. And hurt more.

"Arlie? What's wrong?"

"I...I don't know," said Arlie.

His hands went to his head. It just hurt, that was all. It just hurt. It was like something was squeezing. His toque was squeezing. The toque! Mrs. Spinx's toque!

Arlie pulled it off. An immediate feeling of physical relief swept over him. He looked at the toque in disgust. And then he smiled. He couldn't help it. Inside the toque, worked into the pattern of the wool itself, was a single word.

Pinhead.

What a strange word to find inside a togue knitted by a little old lady.

Wasn't that Jan's word for Mr. Vanderguard?

And was this how you got to be a pinhead? By being mad at everything all the time? Even your friends?

The word seemed to be fading back into the pattern of the wool. Maybe Arlie had imagined it. He tested to size of the hat against his hands. It seemed a regular-sized toque again. Maybe he had imagined that too.

Maybe, but he wasn't taking any chances.

He put the toque in his pocket; then he turned back to Jan.

"O.K.," he said. "O.K. Maybe you did the right thing. Maybe I was dumb not to at least tell someone where I was going. At least we're here and we've still got some time. There seems to be someone at home in the apartment beside his. Let's ask there."

"Next door. He lives next door," said the man who answered their ring. "But he won't be home now. He'll be down at the hotel. He runs the hotel for the owners in the winter while they go to Florida. It's only in the summer that he runs the fishing store in the Market."

"Which hotel?" asked Jan.

"The one on Main Street. The Timberliner."

Jan and Arlie looked at each other.

"A tall man?" asked Jan. "Tall and fair?"

The man nodded.

"Cigarette hanging out the side of his mouth?" asked Arlie. "Eyes that look in two different directions?"

"What? Oh no, Curly doesn't smoke. That must be Frank. Dear no, not Frank. Frank does odd jobs and sweeps up, runs the bottles down to the depot. You know, they kind of look after him. But no, he's not the one you want. Curly wears a cowboy shirt. He'll be back in the office somewhere."

Jan and Arlie looked at each other with much relief and headed down back to town.

Chapter 9

In the end Arlie surprised himself. He just walked right in and said, "Hello, my name is Arlie Zack and my mom's name is Sandy and I think you're my dad."

The man's mouth opened and 57 emotions passed over his face. It was wonderful to see in a way but frightening too. Arlie was afraid for a moment Curly simply was going to deny it all and Arlie wasn't sure he could take that. But his father didn't. When the emotions had run their course, he looked away for a moment. He looked around the room and out the window and then he shook his head and looked back at Arlie.

"I guess I am," he said. "Hello, Arlie."

And he put out his hand.

It wasn't the best greeting in the world, but as they shook hands, Arlie knew it was all he wanted for now. He didn't want hugs or explanations or fantastic greetings. The man across from him was a stranger—and, as with any stranger, you started from scratch, feeling around the edges.

They went for lunch at a restaurant across the street. Arlie had noticed that about adults. When they didn't know what else to do, they fed you, but that was O.K. because Arlie was pretty hungry by then anyway, and he guessed Jan was too. They'd gotten through the basics by then

—no, his mom wasn't along

—yes, he and his friend had just come especially to see him. They'd found him by the article in "Fishing West" magazine. Arlie had been reading fishing magazines for a lot of years now, ever since he'd been given the old fishing trophy with his dad's name on it. He'd been reading fishing magazines...not really even hoping, but just in case.

About halfway through the hamburgers two policemen came into the restaurant and settled down to coffee at the counter. From the way they looked around the room every now and then, Arlie had a feeling they weren't there by accident. He began to get anxious. He expected his dad to get up and slip out the back door. Instead, when the policemen caught his eye, his dad nodded at them across the room.

"Seems to me you're being watched over," said his dad.

"Me?" said Arlie. "Aren't they after you?"

His dad looked perplexed.

"But...I mean...are you still in trouble... "

An uncomfortable understanding came into his dad's eyes.

"That was cleared up a long time ago, Arlie. It was my own fault for running in the first place. I hadn't done anything wrong, except hang out with a bunch of the wrong people, but I guess you wouldn't know that. I guess your mother wouldn't know that either."

"You mean you didn't run off to the Bahamas or something because they were after you?"

"I did and I didn't. I ran off, but it wasn't really me they wanted. And when they found that out...I was clear to come back."

"But you didn't try to find us?"

"I did, but you were gone," said his dad.

Arlie could feel all the old anger in him. So it was his mom's fault!

But his dad was looking into his coffee cup and scowling.

"No that's not quite true. I guess if you went to the trouble to look for me you deserve the truth. I tried to find you... once...a little...but I didn't try very hard. I'm sure if I'd tried really hard, I'd have found you. There were enough leads. I'm sorry, Arlie. I had a lot of problems. Your mom and I weren`t getting along very well—we hadn't gotten along for quite a while in fact. It was mostly my fault. And maybe I was just a coward. I talked myself into believing it was better for everyone if I didn't find you. Everyone...especially me.

"But I'll tell you one thing. Right at this moment I'm feeling I made the wrong choice. If I hadn't run, maybe I'd have realized what a good thing it could be to have a son like you."

It hurt, but Arlie could take it.

"Look, what are your plans?" asked his dad.

"For what?" asked Arlie.

"For now. Today. Tomorrow," said his dad.

Today. Tomorrow. The day after tomorrow. Arlie knew it was time to make up his own mind.

"I'm going home on the evening bus," he said.

"Shall we tell them that?" asked his dad. "It might make things easier."

Arlie nodded. His dad slipped over and talked to the policemen.

"I like him," said Jan.

"I do too," said Arlie.

Things were easier after that. Arlie's dad had to be at the hotel all afternoon, so Arlie and Jan hung around with him there. They played desk clerk and answered the telephone and added up the receipts. It wasn't very busy. Arlie's dad even had time to tie a few fishing flies at the small desk he had set up for that purpose at the back of the office. As he wrapped and knotted and tied minute feathers into place he told Arlie how, after he'd come back to Canada, he had tried several things before finally settling here in Raven.

"I guess some people are born for the big city life, and some aren't," he said. "I don't get rich here but I don't get in trouble either." He tied two tiny loops of thread, snipped, released the iridescent green fly from the clamp and held it up with a pair of tweezers. "And I tie one heck of a 52 Buick. Would you like it?"

"I...I don't fish," said Arlie.

His dad looked totally disconcerted.

"But I could stick it in the side of my hat. Some of the kids at school do that."

"Sure, why not," said his dad.

When it came time for the evening bus, Jan said she'd get a seat for both of them and hopped quickly on board. Arlie and his dad stood on the veranda of the hotel watching the driver sort and load his freight parcels. Arlie knew it was time to go, but all he could do was stand there.

"He's about ready I think," said his dad, and took a step down the stairs. Still Arlie didn't move. His dad turned back to him. His eyes looked steadily into Arlie's own.

"It doesn't have to be goodbye, Arlie. I don't know what your mom will say...and I can't speak for you either. But I'm not running away any more—especially not now!"

Arlie couldn't help himself then. He hugged his dad, and felt his dad hug him back. With a sudden feeling of buoyancy he raced down to the bus.

Jan's mom and Arlie's mom were both waiting by the bus depot.

"I hope you don't get in a lot of trouble," said Arlie.

"So do I," said Jan.

Arlie and his mom walked home together. His mom had her arm around his shoulder. Arlie didn't try to shrug it off.

"Are you mad at me?" he asked

"I'm just glad you're back," his mother answered.

"Mom..."

"I was frightened, Arlie. Frightened you were gone for good. Frightened something would happen to you that you couldn't handle. There are so many rotten things that can happen to a kid your age out there, Arlie. You can't just go taking off. You're only twelve years old, for crying out loud..."

Arlie didn't answer.

His mom took a deep breath and looked up into the darkness where big flakes of snow drifted silently down to meet them.

"What I really am is sorry, Arlie," she said. "I'm sorry because if I'd at least left some sort of a door open, so you could have felt you could talk to me about your dad..."

"I like him, Mom," said Arlie. "At least I think I do."

His mom nodded.

"You can see him again and find out for sure," she said. "If you want to. If he wants to. But you have to be part of it too, Arlie. You have to talk. You have to let people know what's going on in your mind. For better or for worse, you've got to at least tell the people close to you. Even complicated things can be worked out."

Arlie knew, now, his mother was telling the truth. He wondered how hard it had been for her not to come racing down to Raven herself to bring him back. He wondered what she would have done if Pete hadn't been around to quietly help out. He figured she would have found another way.

"There's something else I have to talk to you about," said Arlie. "About some kids at school."

Chapter 10

"Arlie Zack to the office, Arlie Zack."

The boom has just dropped, thought Arlie. All morning he'd been trying to screw up his courage to talk to Mrs. Scott about the things that had happened with C.J. and Clinton. After discussing it with his mom he'd decided that was the only thing to do, really. At least he trusted Mrs. Scott not to make it bigger than it was. Now the game was up and if Vanderguard had turned him in Arlie wasn't sure what was going to happen. Vanderguard had a mean streak.

But when he got to the office he knew it couldn't have been Vanderguard who'd blown the whistle. Vanderguard hadn't seen C.J. or

Clinton, yet there they sat on the bench outside the principal's office. Their faces were white. Arlie was pretty sure his face was white too. He sat down a little apart from them, and, as he did so, a large woman with spiked orange hair and heavy blue eyeshadow came out of the principal's office. She paused dramatically in the doorway, glanced at the boys and then said loudly over her shoulder back into the office.

"Two dozen eggs one day, 5 pounds of sugar the next. What did he suppose I'd think he was doing...baking a cake?"

She gave the three boys a withering look and clacked off down the hall in her high heels. At the corner she stopped to explain it all again to one of the secretaries.

"Who is that?" asked Arlie.

"My mother," said C.J.

Arlie felt sorry for C.J. Arlie's mother was a bit embarrassing with her jewellery and skateboarding and philosophies, but at least she wasn't loud about it. And at least she'd given Arlie the chance to turn himself in.

The session in the principal's office didn't take long. Arlie was a little surprised that Mrs. Lu had figured the church window breakage with the rest, but she'd been principal a long time, so maybe she just automatically recognized the pattern.

The sentence included full written apologies all around, payment to the church, and complete washing of all windows—inside and out—of the church, Mrs. Scott's house, Mr. Vanderguard's house and the entire school.

It was recess by the time the boys filed out of the office. The three of them went to a little-used part of the schoolyard and leaned with their backs against the brick wall.

Silently.

"I don't get it, Zack," said C.J. at last. "Why didn't you tell Mrs. Lu you weren't in on it? I mean you were there, but you never did anything. She might have let you off."

Arlie didn't answer. All questions didn't have to have answers. It was something he was learning.

"With only two of us it would have taken us forever to wash all those windows," said Clinton.

Arlie knew it was as close as Clinton was going to come to saying thanks.

"Except I figure someone around here owes the corner store about two dollars for all the sour balls they've been snatching," said Arlie.

C.J. reached in his pocket and handed Arlie the money.

"You give it to them. They'd never believe me. Say your mom went home with a loaf of bread she didn't pay for by mistake or something."

Arlie took the money and nodded. He felt suddenly very tired. It had been a long week. The longest week in his life probably.

For the rest of the day he just kind of hung in there, thinking. He was still trying to figure it all out—C.J., Clinton, Jan and the bus ride and his father—as he headed over to Mrs. Spinx's house after school to shovel the walk.

As he approached the little house beneath the big trees, he couldn't help but wonder how much its occupant had had to do with the changes that had taken place in his life over the past few days. A rock, a sea shell, a puzzle, a hat—Arlie knew in his heart that the gifts Mrs. Spinx had given him weren't magic, at least not the kind of magic that makes fantastic things happen with the speed of lightning. They had to do with the other kind of magic, the simple strength that everyone has inside them if they only get a chance to let it grow. With a little luck it helped a person handle what life turned up without becoming totally lost along the way.

What Arlie didn't understand was how a little old lady like Mrs. Spinx could have known how hard it was to be twelve and looking for answers.

Max was standing on the walk waiting for him.

"I don't like it," said Max.

"What?" asked Arlie.

"I don't like it at all. It doesn't feel right. Do you know what day this is?" asked Max.

"Friday," said Arlie.

"And every Friday Mrs. Spinx goes out at four o'clock to play bingo. But look—do you see any tracks on the walk?"

"No," said Arlie.

"That's right. And last night I was out sweeping just to keep things clean and she didn't go out either. And the same light's been on in her house all day long. Mrs. Spinx doesn't leave lights on in the daytime."

"Maybe she went to visit someone," said Arlie.

"Nope," said Max. "Whenever she goes visiting she leaves the key with Mrs. Cox across the street and Mrs. Cox hangs it on a nail over the window, but there's no key."

Arlie looked across the street at Mrs. Cox's house.

"Max, how do you know all this?" asked Arlie.

"I do. That's all."

Arlie went up to the house and knocked on the back door. He knocked louder. He tried to peek in but couldn't see.

Max and Arlie looked at each other.

"We could go get my mom," said Arlie.

"Let's phone her from my place," said Max.

A half hour later Arlie, Max and Arlie's mom were on the walk outside the house again. They'd arrived with a feeling of something accomplished—Arlie's mom had been able to reach Mrs. Spinx's son in the town an hour's drive away and he'd said he'd come right over with the key. Now, they weren't so sure. An hour suddenly seemed like an eternity and as the sky settled down upon them with the promise of yet another heavy snowfall that might close the roads, Arlie became even more restless.

"I'll go in through the basement," he said. "Mrs. Spinx leaves the window unlocked. She told me that herself. I don't think she'd mind. I mean, we could call the police I suppose, but we don't really know anything's wrong and that could take time. Maybe time is important."

Mrs. Zack considered this for a moment.

"But I'm the one who should go in," she said.

"I don't think you'll fit," said Arlie. "It's an awfully little window."

"Are you sure you want to, Arlie? You never know..."

"It's O.K.," said Arlie.

"I'll go with him," said Max. "I thought we might have to, so I brought these from home."

He reached in his pockets and took out two bulky items—a flashlight and a large, thick ball of string.

Chapter 11

"'50 metres'," read Max off the end of the roll. "I sure hope it's enough."

Max and Arlie were standing on the hard earthen floor of the basement, just inside the little window. Max had tied the end of the string to the window latch and was beginning to unwind it as Arlie used the flashlight to reveal what lay ahead of them.

It was a very cluttered basement—boxes and crates piled one upon another, old clothes hanging from the low ceiling, a phonograph and records along one wall, old furniture resting like lumpy statues. There was too much stuff to even see where the stairs leading up to the house were.

"Max, the whole house probably isn't 150 metres—even if you walked around the outside of it," said Arlie.

"You never know," said Max.

Arlie shook his head but he didn't argue. Looking at the maze before them, he was beginning to feel that having a string to lead them back to the window "just in case" might not be a bad idea after all. Crazy, but not bad.

"Come on," said Arlie. "I think the basement stairs go down from the kitchen. That's this way."

Together they began to wind their way through the piles and lumps and overhangings. Arlie was in the lead. Max followed behind, paying out the string.

"Hey, here's an old miners' lamp," said Max.

"How's that for a saw? It's as big as I am," said Arlie.

"Hats. Look at all these hats," said Max.

"And here's three cases of cranberry juice," said Arlie.

"Oh, oh," said Max.

"Oh, oh, is right," said Arlie, giving the flashlight a shake. "Max, are these old batteries in here?"

"I put new ones in just before I went out star watching," said Max.

"When was that?" asked Arlie.

"Six weeks ago. I went out about 10 times. You should have seen the northern lights. One night I must have stayed out for about three hours," said Max.

"With the flashlight on," said Arlie.

"On and off," said Max.

"Max, I think these batteries are giving up," said Arlie.

"Oh, oh," said Max.

"Come on. We should be able to see the stairs," said Arlie.

In the last fading glow that Arlie aimed across the basement they were just able to see the far wall and a set of stairs leading up. Then the light dimmed and died.

Dark.

Very dark.

"Max?"

"Yeah?"

"You still got hold of the string?"

"You bet."

"Good."

Dark.

Very Dark.

"Max?"

"Yeah?"

"Where are you?"

"Right here," said Max.

He put a hand on Arlie's shoulder. Arlie turned and peered into the darkness.

"It's so dark down here I can't even see you," said Arlie.

"I know," said Max. "You take the ball of string and I'll hold on behind you. That way we're kind of hooked together and if one of us drops it the other will still have it."

"Good idea," said Arlie. He felt Max feeling from his shoulder down to his arm and putting the ball in his hand. It was about half the size Arlie remembered it. Could they really have come that far?

"O.K.," said Arlie. "I think the staircase is just over here."

"I'm right behind you," said Max.

Groping their way this time, fumbling and half tripping and feeling in the dark, they made their way forward until they seemed to hit a wall. Along the wall to the left Arlie felt a clear rise.

"I think we're here," said Arlie. "The stairs are pretty narrow, so watch it."

Up they climbed. Up and up. The string was paying off the roll at a frightening pace, but here was a door. And a handle. Arlie turned the knob and pushed. No good. He turned the knob and stepped back, pulling the door towards him.

Sunlight, brilliant sunlight, blinded their eyes. Both boys blinked hard against the glare. And there was something else too. Warmth. Summer warmth. And smells, soft and warm.

"Max," breathed Arlie.

"I don't want to look," said Max.

"But it's summer," said Arlie. "We're outside and it's summer. It's Mrs. Spinx's yard. The trees aren't big enough, but the gate is the same. No, it's almost the same but newer. And it's summer, Max!"

Arlie took a step higher to look fully out the door.

"And the street outside is dirt, Max. And they're building a house across the street. Out of logs, Max. With a horse and a wagon..."

Arlie stopped. He was beginning to understand what he was saying.

"Max..."

"Wrong door," said Max.

"But Max. Horse and wagon. And there's a girl, Max—about our age, in old-fashioned clothes. She's running this way, Max. She's looking for something. Max, she looks like..."

Max was pulling him back into the basement.

"Close the door," said Max. "Wrong door."

"But it was the past, Max. The past!" said Arlie.

"Don't tell me," said Max. "I don't want to know."

"But the past!" Arlie was amazed.

"Later," said Max. "It's the present we're worried about. We need to find another door."

"We're almost out of string," said Arlie.

"We'll backtrack," said Max. "Wind it up as we go. It'll give us another chance."

Down the stairway they tumbled, to the earthen floor. Along the wall they moved, until they reached another set of stairs. Up. Up. Another door.

"You go this time," said Arlie.

"No way," said Max. "I'm strictly backup."

Arlie took hold of the doorknob and slowly, carefully pulled it towards him so the door opened just a crack. He peered through. He saw linoleum—green patterned linoleum, brighter and flatter than he remembered it but the same pattern as in Mrs. Spinx's kitchen. He opened the door another crack. He could see legs—table legs, people legs. He looked up. People were sitting down to supper. A family—

the man with his shirt sleeves rolled up, the woman in a print dress, four young boys with curly chestnut hair. There was cake...it seemed to be someone's birthday. As the woman leaned across the table the strong fine lines of her face were illuminated softly by the light of candles.

Arlie closed the door.

"Better," he said. "Closer, I think. But not yet."

Down the stairs again into the darkness. Looking, looking. How long had they been down here? Was he frightened? No, he was amazed.

Up the stairs again. A door. Arlie found the knob and stopped. He could hear voices inside.

"This handle is made of bone, now, Arlie. You don't see that anymore. It was given to me on my wedding day by my Aunt Triss. Poor as a church mouse but she gave me four bone-handled knives. And, oh, she was so kind, was my Aunt Triss."

"What's wrong?" asked Max.

"It's a couple of days ago," said Arlie, "when I was here overnight! That's when it is, Max! Why if it can be shaved so close then there must be millions of doors. For millions of days. Maybe one for each second of each minute of each day. We'll never find..."

"No, it's all right," said Max. "We're getting closer. Listen."

Arlie listened. It was a tapping, a far off knocking, the kind of knocking you might make as a signal. A signal for help.

Down the stairs in darkness again, but this time not alone. The knocking was getting louder.

"This way," said Arlie.

Yes, it was louder. Stairs again. And this time, looking up ahead of him, Arlie could see a thin band of light like that which squeaks through the bottom of the door.

The knocking was louder, more definite. That thin band of light gave Arlie hope. He reached the door, felt for the knob and slowly opened it.

The linoleum this time was worn and rolling. Arlie looked higher. He saw the table, small and pushed against the wall, the way he remembered it from his visit. Above it was a calendar. February. February 1993. Yes, yesterday had been the first of February. And the tapping was very real.

"This is it," said Arlie.

"Are you sure?" asked Max.

"I hope so," said Arlie.

He took a step into the room. One step. Two steps. Where was the knocking coming from?

"Max, come quick!"

Mrs. Spinx was lying on the floor just inside the living room. She must have been getting ready to go out, for she'd pulled her big coat down over her, but she did not seem to be able to rise. In her hand was her cane with which she was still knocking, knocking. She did not seem even to see Arlie as he reached over and gently laid it aside.

"We're here, Max and I," he said. "We'll get help."

The old lady closed her eyes and lay very still.

Chapter 12

It did not snow again that winter in Arlie's town. As the snow shrank and spring began to work its way into the air the old people passing on the street nodded and said they deserved it after that week at the end of January when it snowed so heavily for so many days in a row.

The air warmed. The greens began to show in earth and tree with a promise that reminded Arlie of a door opening.

It was a busy spring for Arlie, and not necessarily an easy one. The window washing went slowly and it wasn't always easy working things out with his dad.

School, however, had ceased to be a

problem. Arlie wasn't ever going to be the best student in school, but he found it a lot easier to get along now that he wasn't angry the way he had been.

And Max, and Jan? Well, at first C.J. and Clinton had looked at Arlie as if he was crazy whenever they ran into him helping Max mow lawns. And they'd looked at him as if he was double crazy when he told them he'd spent the afternoon sitting up in some tree with Jan helping her memorize words out of a dictionary. Arlie didn't care. Arlie figured friends are friends. They come in all varieties and Arlie liked it that way.

It wasn't until May that Arlie heard that Mrs. Spinx was coming home from the hospital.

"At least her son is going to try and bring her home for a few hours to see if he can't get her interested in things again," said Arlie's mom. "The stroke affected her walking for a while but she's much better now. The trouble is…well, she seems to have become removed from… living."

"What do you mean?" asked Arlie.

"I don't know if I can describe it better," said his mom. "She just doesn't seem to care any more. She's quite a lady, you know. It's sad to think of someone like that just giving up, especially when the doctor says she's still strong physically."

Arlie was there when the car drove up the next day to the little white house beneath the trees. He watched an older man, balding but with a bush of curly chestnut hair at the back, climb out of the car and come around to the passenger side. He spoke through the open window, looked around him, gestured at the trees and flowers, spoke again.

Mrs. Spinx, however, did not get out. After a few minutes the man strolled off into the yard on his own.

Arlie took a deep breath and started along the sidewalk.

"Hello, Mrs. Spinx," said Arlie, coming even with the open car window.

Mrs. Spinx turned to look at him. The recognition was slow in her grey eyes.

"Arlie," she said. "Hello, Arlie."

"I hear you might be coming home for a while today," said Arlie.

"Oh, I don't think so," she said. "I'm old, you know."

"I know," said Arlie. "You're 210."

A little light of remembering showed behind the greyness.

"Anyway, remember those things you gave me for shovelling your walk? The rock? And the conch? Remember the toque?"

Mrs. Spinx didn't answer.

"Well, I've got something for you too," said Arlie.

He reached into his pocket and brought out a small stick.

"It's a pointer," he said, holding it out to her in the palm of his hand. "You point it the way you want to go and then you go there."

It sounded so utterly ridiculous that Arlie almost sank through the sidewalk. How could he have even tried. How could he have even thought...

But Mrs. Spinx had picked it up between her own fingers. It was the nicest kind of small stick, really. Arlie had found it along the river. The water had smoothed it and shaped it and there was an interesting swirl in the grain of the wood that was like an eye.

"This stick is pointed on both ends," said Mrs. Spinx.

"I know," said Arlie.

"You do?"

"Oh, yes," said Arlie.

The old lady closed her fist upon the little bit of smooth wood for a moment, rolling it in her hand, feeling the grain of life that it held still, thinking. Then slowly, slowly, she uncurled her fingers. There lay Arlie's stick.

"Pointed at both ends," she said.

"I didn't want to take any chances," said Arlie. "I'm only an amateur at this."

The briefest of smiles passed over Mrs. Spinx's face, rapidly followed by something of greater substance.

Arlie opened the door. Mrs. Spinx climbed slowly out of the car. She took the cane and straightened and took a deep breath, looking around her, taking in all the sights and sounds and maybe the memories as well. Who knew what memories were there for her to see? But it wasn't really the past Mrs. Spinx was thinking about.

"Your mom tells me you go fishing with your dad these days," she said, turning slightly towards Arlie.

"Yup," said Arlie.

"I never knew my own father very well," said Mrs. Spinx. "He was killed in a mining accident when I was quite young. But if I had known him, I think I would have enjoyed going fishing with him very much. Very much indeed."

Then she smacked Arlie on the shin with her cane to move him out of the way, and set off determinedly along the sidewalk to her home.